Extreme Sports No Limits!

Extreme Climbing

John Crossingham & Bobbie Kalman

Crabtree Publishing Company

www.crabtreebooks.com

Created by Bobbie Kalman

Dedicated by Rob MacGregor
For Monkey-Man Jim. Ape factor plus!

Editor-in-Chief
Bobbie Kalman

Writing team
John Crossingham
Bobbie Kalman

Substantive editor
Amanda Bishop

Project editor
Kelley MacAulay

Editors
Molly Aloian
Rebecca Sjonger
Kathryn Smithyman

Art director
Robert MacGregor

Design
Katherine Kantor

Production coordinator
Heather Fitzpatrick

Photo research
Crystal Foxton

Consultants
John Owen, American Alpine Club Library Committee
Maggie Owen, Mountaineering Historian

Photographs
Karl Baba: pages 4, 10, 11, 15 (top), 16, 31
Denver Public Library, Western History Collection,
 W.H. Jackson, WHJ 1902: page 6
© Paul Martinez/Photosport.com: page 27
Shazamm: pages 7, 26, 28, 29
Other images by Corbis Images, Digital Stock, and PhotoDisc

Illustrations
Katherine Kantor: pages 8, 9, 12-13

Digital prepress
Embassy Graphics

Printer
Worzalla Publishing Company

Crabtree Publishing Company

www.crabtreebooks.com   1-800-387-7650

PMB 16A	612 Welland Avenue	73 Lime Walk
350 Fifth Avenue	St. Catharines	Headington
Suite 3308	Ontario	Oxford
New York, NY	Canada	OX3 7AD
10118	L2M 5V6	United Kingdom

Cataloging-in-Publication Data
Kalman, Bobbie.
 Extreme climbing / Bobbie Kalman & John Crossingham.
  p. cm. -- (Extreme sports - no limits)
 Includes index.
  ISBN 0-7787-1671-6 (RLB) -- ISBN 0-7787-1717-8 (pbk.)
 1. Rock climbing--Juvenile literature. 2. Extreme sports--Juvenile
literature. [1. Rock climbing. 2. Extreme sports.] I. Crossingham,
John. II. Title. III. Extreme sports no limits!
 GV200.2.K34 2004
 796.52'23--dc22
                                                              2003027235
                                                              LC

CONTENTS

In the sport of rock climbing, people make their way up rock **faces**, or vertical surfaces, by gripping the rock with their hands and by balancing on their feet. Rock climbing is an **individual** sport, or a sport in which athletes perform alone, but most rock climbers climb with a partner or in a group. They learn to use equipment and specific body positions to travel up and down steep rock faces. Rock climbing can be done on rocks that are hundreds of feet tall or those that are not far off the ground.

THE EXTREME CHALLENGE

Climbing is a daring sport that requires training, confidence, and strength. The rock faces favored by many climbers are very steep and dangerous—so dangerous that climbing is considered an **extreme sport**. Extreme sports push athletes to the limits of their abilities. Some climbers risk their lives for their sport! Many of the best climbers are **professionals**—they get paid to climb. Other great climbers are simply daring people who love a challenge.

Rock climbers use skill and courage to conquer amazing heights.

EXTREME DANGER ⚠

The climbers featured in this book are experts with years of experience and training behind them. Any type of climbing is very dangerous and requires proper equipment and instruction. Do not attempt anything in this book without adult supervision. For more information on safety, see pages 8-11.

Artificial climbing walls and boulders are specially constructed surfaces that enable people to climb indoors.

WHAT KIND OF CLIMB?

Each style of climbing involves different techniques, equipment, and surfaces. **Traditional climbing** or "trad" is a style of climbing in which athletes place **anchors** in the rock face as they move upward. In **sport climbing**, athletes climb for speed on rock faces with pre-placed anchors.

Bouldering, one of the most challenging types of climbing, is just like rock climbing, except the climbers do not use any ropes or **harnesses**. In **ice climbing**, athletes use picks and special boots to climb sheer faces of solid ice, such as frozen waterfalls. These styles of rock climbing are covered on pages 20-25.

UPWARD AND ONWARD

The first rock climbers were **mountaineers**, or mountain explorers. In the early 1860s, a few bold mountaineers climbed slopes that were steeper than average hiking trails. These early climbers had very few guides to help them learn to climb. Instead, they traded knowledge and advice with one another and began to invent ways of solving climbing problems.

SOMETHING TO WORK WITH

Before long, people all over the world were experimenting with rock climbing. Climbers invented new tools and created new techniques. In the 1930s, they started wedging **chockstones**, or small rocks, into cracks on the rock face. They then tied ropes to the chockstones to help them climb. Soon, stronger metal **nuts** were invented. By the 1960s, these tools helped climbers attempt more difficult climbs. Through the 1960s and 1970s, equipment such as harnesses and **bolts** were introduced. With this gear, climbers reached new heights.

FREE TO FALL

As some climbers were designing climbing equipment, other climbers were giving up equipment altogether! In the 1950s, a native of Boulder, Colorado named John Gill created the climbing style now known as "bouldering." To climb, he used nothing but his hands and feet! **Free** climbers began using ropes only as a safety precaution, not to get up the rock face. **Solo** climbers even left their climbing partners behind—they climbed all alone!

NOT JUST FOR EXPERTS

In the 1970s, the artificial climbing wall introduced the sport to a new audience. Not only were climbing walls the safest places to climb, but they could be set up almost anywhere. Indoor climbing became popular as a challenging workout at gyms. In the 1990s, the extreme sports craze made all styles of climbing even more popular. Climbing became recognized as an extreme athletic challenge, alongside other extreme sports such as BMX, skateboarding, and surfing.

CLIMBING'S COUSIN

Some climbers combined new climbing techniques with traditional hiking and **scrambling** in order to conquer giant mountains such as Mount Everest. Many climbers still practice this style, now known as **alpine climbing**.

ROCK GEAR

The equipment used by climbers varies from one style to the next, but all climbers need proper gear. Safety helmets and comfortable weather-appropriate clothing are absolutely necessary.

helmet

A backpack is used to carry extra items on longer climbs.

A climber's jacket should be light, as well as windproof and waterproof, to protect against chilly wind and rain.

HARD AS ROCK

Climbing **helmets** can help prevent injury to a climber's head during a fall. The **shells**, or outer casings, of helmets are made from a variety of lightweight materials such as **fiberglass** and plastic. The **lining**, or inside of the helmet, is padded foam. Helmets also have adjustable chin straps that keep them in place in any situation.

*A **chalkbag** holds chalk dust, which climbers rub on their hands to improve their grip on the rock.*

To prepare for temperature changes, climbers often wear layers of clothing, including climbing tights, vests, T-shirts, and shorts.

Gloves are worn to protect the hands when handling ropes, but they are not worn during rock climbing.

Rock boots have soft rubber soles that grip the rock face. The boots are also designed to fit into narrow grooves in rock.

ALL TIED UP

A rope is sometimes the only thing that prevents a falling climber from hitting the ground. Climbing rope is designed to handle a lot of stress. It comes in lengths of 164 or 197 feet (50 or 60 m). Most ropes are about three-eighths of an inch (1 cm) thick. Climbers must be able to tie solid knots in rope. The knots attach the ropes to one another or to anchors.

gear loop

leg loop

STRAPPED IN

Climbers use harnesses to attach themselves to ropes. A harness is a belt with **leg loops**, or loops of fabric through which climbers put their legs. It allows climbers to hang in a stable, seated position. Harnesses also have **gear loops**, or loops of fabric that keep equipment within easy reach.

ROPED IN

Ropes are necessary for most types of climbing, but they aren't much good on their own. Several devices help hold ropes in place and make them easier to use on the rock face.

rope

hex

Hexes *are locked inside oddly shaped cracks.*

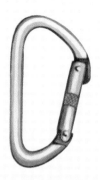

Ropes and **slings** *are connected using clips called* **carabiners** *or "biners." These clips can be either snapped or screwed shut.*

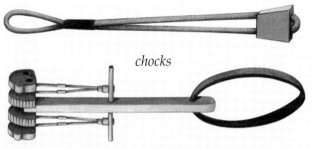

chocks

To connect ropes to rock, climbers use a variety of anchors. **Chocks** *are wedged inside cracks to provide a firm anchor. Many chocks come with small nylon or wire slings already attached.*

PLAYING IT SAFE

*Most climbers have a love of nature. They protect the environment surrounding climbing areas. Climbers are careful to clean up **routes**, or paths, as they climb them. They remove old equipment and clean chalk off ledges.*

Some climbs are performed in high, remote areas. The weather can change quickly in these difficult-to-reach places. Climbers must be prepared to handle bad weather or nasty accidents during a climb. Devices such as radios or cellular phones can allow a climber in trouble to contact rescuers. Matches, flashlights, food, water, blankets, and a first-aid kit are all items that can save a stranded or injured climber's life.

PROPER BEHAVIOR

Safety equipment helps keep athletes out of harm's way, but safety goes beyond equipment. Climbers follow many rules and follow a code of **ethics**, or respectful behavior, in order to make climbing sites safe and welcoming places.

THE GANG'S ALL HERE

Most people climb in a group of at least two people. The group members assist one another and provide help in case of an emergency. The most experienced climber in a group is generally chosen as the leader. The leader may climb in the lead position to help set up the route of the climb.

SLEEPING ON THE JOB

Some climbs, often called **big wall** climbs, take more than one day to complete. Whenever a climb lasts longer than a day, climbers must bring enough gear to **bivouac**, or camp in an unsheltered area. This gear includes food, extra clothing, and safety tools. Climbers sleep in sleeping bags that hang from a climbing rope, or they use a **portaledge**, which is a frame that bolts into the rock face and acts as a cot.

Being the leader is a big responsibility because this person must be able to organize the climb.

Climbers are able to attach a portaledge to the rock face. This equipment allows them to sleep during a long climb.

11

FEATURE PRESENTATION

Every rock face is different, but they all share common **features**, or distinct parts. To make these features easy to recognize, climbers have given them names. Some features, such as **aretes** and **overhangs**, jut out from the rock face. Others, such as **corners** and **grooves**, curve inward. Features may be different sizes and shapes, but all can be used to a climber's advantage. The more uneven the face, the easier it is to climb. Several countries also have their own **rating systems** that tell climbers how difficult a rock is to climb. Ratings often include a **grade**, or a number that states roughly how dangerous the climb will be.

1. Overhangs are places where the rock juts out horizontally.

*2. A **nose** is an outward-pointing mound on the rock face.*

*3. A **chimney** is a narrow corner or a point where two walls almost face each other.*

4. Grooves are small corners that are often rounded.

*5. **Cracks** are narrow breaks in the rock.*

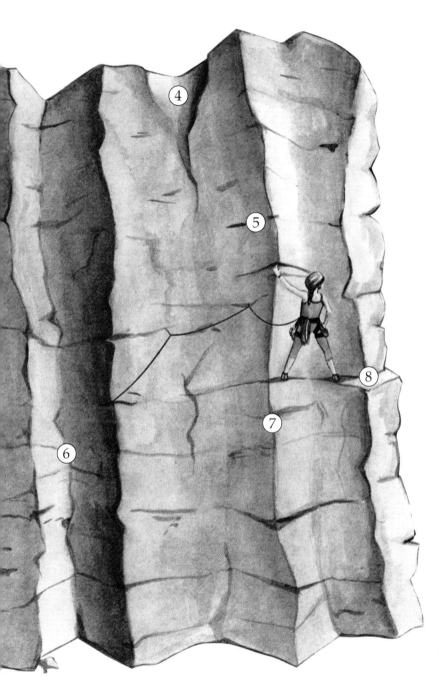

6. A corner is an inward angle on the rock face.

7. Aretes point out from the rock face at an angle.

*8. A **ledge** is a small shelf that a climber can grip.*

THIS ROCK IS NOT YET RATED

The American climbing rating system ranges from 1 to 6. Levels 1 and 2 are quite flat and suitable for walking and hiking. Level 3 means that scrambling is needed. A rating of 4 means that the slope is dangerous and rope should be used. All rock faces that are ranked 5 require technical climbing skills. A 6 face is so smooth and steep that it is impossible to climb!

NUMBER 5

Not all faces with a rating of 5 are the same. The 5 scale goes from 5.0 (the least difficult 5) to 5.14d (the most difficult 5). There are additional numbers and sometimes letters that describe how difficult a climb is. A rock face rated 5.12 is extremely difficult. A 5.12c is even tougher! Climbers use these rankings to determine whether or not a climb is within their abilities.

GETTING A GRIP

Climbers **ascend**, or move up, and **descend**, or move down, a rock face using features on the rock called **holds**. They grip the holds with their hands and feet. **Handholds** are gripped in different ways, depending on their shapes. Climbers use their fingers, thumbs, and palms to grasp or pinch a ledge, poke into a hole, or wedge into a crack.

They use handholds mainly to stay balanced and steady, so sometimes the rock features are small. Climbers balance on **footholds** by pushing their toes or the inside edge of a foot against the rock face or into a groove. Footholds must be firm because they usually support a climber's full weight.

Rubbing chalk on the hands helps a climber get a firm hold on the rock features.

WITHIN REACH

Good climbers keep their weight evenly balanced and move only one limb at a time. The best holds are within comfortable reach—straining too hard can lead to nasty falls. Climbers test holds before using them by kicking or knocking them. If the holds are stable, they continue with the climb. Sometimes climbers who wish to ascend find that there are no satisfying holds above them. Instead, they must **traverse**, or move sideways, or even descend to locate a better route up the rock face.

ANCHORS AWAY

Climbers also grip chocks, which they wedge inside natural cracks in the rock. A chock is wider on the top end than it is on the bottom. As it slides into a crack, it gets stuck. The harder the climber pulls down on the chock, the tighter the chock is wedged and the stronger the anchor becomes. These anchors are then removed by tapping them up out of the cracks.

Traversing allows climbers to avoid difficult situations and find easier ways up the rock face.

Proper rock boots have excellent soles for gripping tiny footholds.

15

LEARNING THE ROPES

Ropes help climbers safely ascend and descend a rock face. Often, one member of a group guides the rope as another member climbs. This move is called **belaying**. The **belayer** wraps the rope around his or her waist or feeds it through a **belay device**. The rope is then tied to the climber's harness. Belayers support their partners in case of a fall.

SLACK AND LIVE

A belayer's rope has two ends. The **live end** is attached to the climber, and the **slack end** hangs loose. As the climber moves upward, the belayer pulls in the live end to keep the rope tight. A tight rope will keep a climber who slips from falling very far. Some belays are **top belays**, which means the belayer guides the climber from above. **Toproping** is done by attaching the rope to an anchor above the climber while the belayer works below (see page 23).

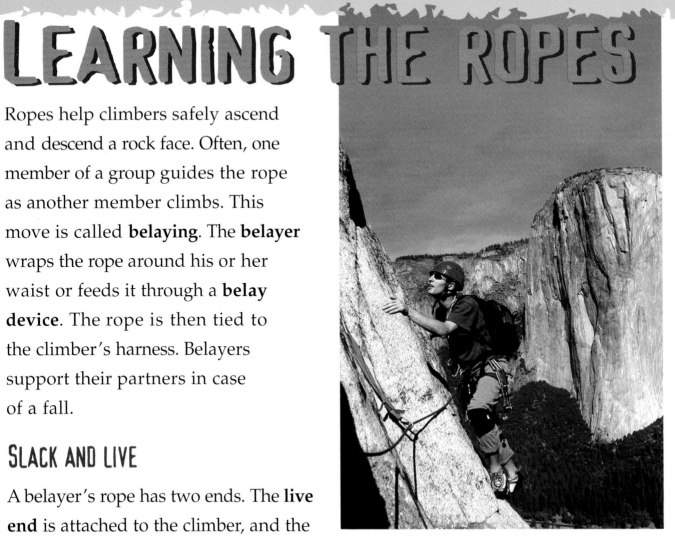

ANCHOR CHAIN
As leaders ascend a rock face, they place anchors a few feet apart along the path. The belay rope is fed through a biner attached to the end of each anchor. Eventually, the leader leaves a series of anchors up the face. These devices provide extra protection in case of a fall because a climber is supported by several anchors.

COMING DOWN

Climbers **rappel**, or slide down a rope, using a **descender**. The descender is attached to the harness to control how quickly the rope moves through the harness. To rappel, climbers place their **upper hand** on the rope above the descender in order to guide the rope. The **controlling hand**, held just under the waist, stops and starts the descent. Climbers slide down by moving the rope away from their bodies. If they move the controlling hand behind their backs, the rope is "braked" and the descent stops.

A descender can even allow climbers to rappel down without touching the rock face.

THE MOVES

Natural cliffs and slopes can have odd formations that challenge climbers. Difficult rock faces require a wide range of skills. Climbers must be able to stretch over wide gaps, move up tight spaces, and get on top of ledges that hang over their heads. To do so, they depend on **pressure** and **friction**. Pressure is created when a climber pulls on or pushes off the rock. Friction is created when two surfaces, such as a rock shoe and a rock face, rub together. These forces, combined with flexibility, strength, and patience, help climbers overcome most obstacles.

LIE-BACKING

When **lie-backing** (shown left), climbers use thin vertical features such as cracks or aretes to get past awkward sections. A climber pulls on the side of the feature with both hands and then leans away from the feature. The feet push against the rock to move upward. Lie-backing is done quickly because it is very tiring.

DYNOS

On occasion, climbers cannot find any holds within reach. They must then make a **dyno**, or a jump to another hold. Before they make the big leap, climbers must be very sure of their targets!

BRIDGING

Sometimes good holds are spaced far apart. Stretching from one hold to another is called **bridging**. To bridge, a climber starts by reaching one hand toward the desired hold. Once that hand is secure, he or she stretches a leg to a solid foothold. Now the climber can move upward or continue to traverse across the rock face.

CHIMNEYING

Chimneying allows climbers to move up chimneys in the rock face. The classic position is with the back flat against one side of the chimney, while the legs are out in front so that the feet push against the other wall. Some chimneys are so thin that the climber is almost standing up straight inside them.

Bridging allows climbers to ascend corners and some chimneys.

THE SPORTING LIFE

Sport climbing allows climbers to practice their techniques on routes that are already set up for them. Sport climbing is safer than most types of climbing, so people with little experience often try it first. Sport climbers don't need much equipment. They use little more than chalk, a harness, rope, and good climbing shoes. As a result, sport climbing has become very popular.

BOLTED IN

A sport-climb route is made up of bolts that are drilled and screwed into the rock ahead of time. These bolts act as permanent anchors. Since the route is already decided, sport climbers tend to move up a face faster than other climbers can.

Although the anchors are bolted in on a sport-climbing route, the paths can be very challenging. Sport routes are designed to test an athlete's skill.

QUICK CLIMBS

When climbers realized how quickly they could move up permanent routes, they began climbing them as fast as they could! **Speed climbing** is sport climbing with a finish line—climbers race along a route and try to get the fastest time. Most speed climbing is done on artificial climbing walls, which are the safest surfaces.

FAKING IT

Climbing walls and indoor climbing gyms rarely look like real rock faces. These colorful climbing courses have many notches and grooves to act as handholds and footholds. The walls also have numerous anchors to make each climb as safe as possible. There may even be a large, soft mat at the base. Although climbing walls are rarely taller than 70 feet (21.3 m), they allow people who do not live near a mountain to try climbing. These walls are sometimes found at fairs and amusement parks as well as at fitness centers.

Many young climbers today do much of their climbing on artificial walls instead of on real rock faces.

HANDS ON

Many climbers consider bouldering to be the greatest test of skill. Boulderers use no ropes or anchors. They depend on their abilities to find and use good holds. This style of climbing greatly improves technical skills. A climber who boulders often has greater strength and better techniques than do other climbers. Climbers work on their skills by bouldering on rocks just above the ground, making short but difficult climbs. Even good climbers must try several times before they succeed. To avoid injury, climbers depend on a large pad of soft foam called a **crash pad,** or on a **spotter**, who is a person that stands under the climber to direct him or her to a soft landing in case of a fall.

GOING SOLO

A few of the best climbers perform only bouldering. Since there are no ropes for belaying, boulderers do not need partners, so they sometimes choose to climb solo. Some daring solo climbers boulder on steep rock faces hundreds of feet in the air. Bouldering is the most dangerous type of climbing because, without any safety gear, even a single mistake can be deadly!

TOP IT OFF

Climbers toprope when they want to get the feel of bouldering with some added safety. To toprope, a rope is fed through an anchor above the climber. A belayer guides the other end of the rope as the climber moves upward. Only one rope and an anchor are used. It may not be real bouldering, but toproping allows a climber to test his or her skills safely.

*In North America, faces used for bouldering are ranked using the **Roman numeral** V and a digit. V1 represents the easiest boulder, and V14 stands for the toughest.*

SLIPPERY SURFACES

Ice climbing is similar to rock climbing in that it features rope techniques such as rappelling and belaying. Ice climbers also place anchors along their climb routes. However, extremely cold temperatures and slippery, unpredictable surfaces make ice climbing a very different experience. In addition to waterproof and weatherproof snowsuits, ice climbers use a variety of spiky tools to grip frozen slopes.

"ICE" TO SEE YOU

Ice that is extremely thick and hard is best for climbing. It is often found near the tops of high mountains, at frozen waterfalls, or on huge sheets of ice and snow called **glaciers**. Climbers must be cautious if they want to climb ice. Favorite routes can become soft if they get too warm in the sun or after many climbers have used them. The time of year is also important. If it is early in winter, for example, ice that looks strong may be too thin to climb.

Ice climbers often use special ropes that are slightly thinner than regular climbing ropes and have a waterproof coating. Ice climbers may also use two ropes instead of one.

STAY SHARP

Ice climbers cannot use holds on the slippery surfaces. Instead, they carry tools to hook into the ice as they climb. **Ice axes** are hand-held curved picks that climbers lodge into the ice. Climbers use their axes one at a time in the same way a rock climber searches for holds. As the ice gets steeper, climbers swing their axes high and hard over their heads to get a deep grip. Ice climbing boots have short spikes, called **crampons**, attached to their toes and bottoms. To get a grip, climbers simply kick the spikes into the ice. Just as rock climbers do, ice climbers test the grip of their axes or crampons before putting their full weight on them.

TURN THE SCREW

Ice climbers use chocks when they encounter patches of rock on a route. On ice, the climbers use special ice screws as anchors. Whereas rock is impossible to drill into without a machine, ice can be drilled by hand. To use an ice screw, the climbers clear away soft ice and make a small hole with their axes. They then simply place the screw in the hole and twist until it is tight in the ice.

There is a rating system to tell the difficulty of an ice climbing route. A Roman numeral, such as VI, rates the difficulty of the terrain, whereas a digit, such as 4, rates the technical climbing difficulty.

25

CLIMBING COMPETITIONS

Rock climbing is traditionally not a sport in which athletes compete with one another. Getting up a rock face, trying new locations, and planning new routes is challenging enough! Still, competitive climbing has become more common since the 1980s. Events usually include speed climbing, bouldering, ice climbing, and **difficulty** events that test each athlete's skill and techniques.

GAME ON!

Extreme sports organizations such as the **X Games** and the **Junior X Games** feature some of the world's best-known climbing events in both winter and summer. Athletes from around the world compete in these annual competitions. International competitions, including the World Cup, also attract climbers from around the globe. **Sponsorships** and competition prizes allow the best climbers to become professionals who make a living from their sport.

TWIN RACERS

A favorite competition is the speed climb. It takes place on two nearly identical climbing walls that are placed side by side. On these walls, two athletes can race at the same time. On a real rock face, the two routes would be quite different, giving one climber an unfair advantage.

Testing, testing

The difficulty event is extremely tough. It is often held on several different artificial walls. Athletes have to complete each climb in a limited amount of time without falling, while also taking hold of as many features on the walls as possible. The winner is the climber with the best combined results from each course. Bouldering events have similar rules, but climbers don't use ropes and anchors.

Among friends

Climbing also involves **informal**, or unofficial, challenges. Often, climbing clubs challenge members to achieve the most "vertical height" over a certain period of time, ranging from a single day to several months. Still, the greatest challenge in climbing is not out-performing other climbers—it's conquering cliffs! This type of challenge makes climbing a constantly changing, endlessly enjoyable sport.

CLIMB TO THE STARS

In its short history, competitive climbing has produced some exceptional athletes. They may not be as famous as Tony Hawk or Michael Jordan, but these fearless athletes possess incredible speed, courage, and have pinpoint accuracy with their hands and feet. Look out above!

HANS FLORINE

California native Hans Florine is one of the world's great speed climbers. He won gold in the X Games event from 1995 to 1997, and he continues to win championships. Florine also spends time as an on-air commentator for sport climbing. "Hollywood Hans" turns 40 in 2004, showing that even a quick sport like speed climbing is not just about youth.

TORI ALLEN

In 2002, at the age of 14, Tori Allen (shown right) became the first American female to win gold in the X Games sport-climbing event. Allen is great in almost any climbing style, including bouldering, speed, difficulty, and just plain old rock climbing. She even has her own action figure! It's safe to say American climbing hopes rest well on her shoulders.

LIBBY HALL

Australian climber Libby Hall is an inspiration to young climbers. In 2002, at age 11, she set a speed climbing record at the Junior X Games. She also won two gold medals and a silver medal. At the 2003 Junior X Games, she broke her own speed climbing record—and won three gold medals! Hall is the top-ranked female junior climber in the world.

CHRIS BLOCH

Californian speed climber Chris Bloch is well known for his many silver medal wins and his powerful climbing style. Bloch tours the country competing and promoting sport climbing to young athletes. He is a great example of how bouldering can improve a climber's skills. Bouldering gave him better muscle strength, which made him a faster climber.

ETTI HENDRAWATI

Speed climbing gold medalist Etti Hendrawati (shown above wearing yellow) is one of the sport's great young ambassadors. A Muslim born in Indonesia, she competes not in shorts and a shirt, but wearing the traditional attire of her religion. Hendrawati has won competitions all around the world, including the Asian X Games.

ROCK ON!

Climbing is an exhilarating sport. It is also very dangerous and requires perfect concentration and patience. Before the artificial climbing wall was invented in the 1970s, many people thought that rock climbing was only for fearless people. Times have changed, however. New climbers can now learn in a safe environment from trained instructors. Proper supervision and instruction are absolutely essential to a new climber.

STARTING OUT

As a beginner, the best way to start out is by going to a climbing camp. Depending on where you live, the camp may be an outdoor climbing school or an indoor climbing gym. Find an instructor who makes you feel comfortable—you will climb your best if you are relaxed and confident.

Thanks to improvements in safety and instruction, climbers are starting out younger all the time.

WORTH THE MONEY

If you find that you really like climbing, you may want to invest in your own equipment. Climbing gear is worth every penny you spend—after all, it guards your life! Shop at a reliable climbing store and ask a lot of questions. Always be sure that your gear is in the best condition possible and remember to double-check it before every climb.

SO MUCH TO LEARN

Books and computers can't take the place of professional guidance, but they can help you improve your knowledge of rock climbing. Climbing magazines and books provide detailed explanations of techniques, equipment, and new ideas in climbing. Your local library or video store may also have movies about the sport. Websites are a quick and inexpensive way to make new discoveries about climbing.

CLIMBING A WEB

Get your search engine running with these climbing websites:

www.rockclimbing.com—an endless source of info on climbers, location, and equipment
www.allexperts.com/getExpert.asp?Category=2259—ask over twenty experts questions about rock climbing
Go to a search engine and type in "rock climbing" along with another word such as "history" or "kids" to discover all sorts of things about your new favorite sport.

GLOSSARY

Note: Boldfaced words that are defined in the text may not appear in the glossary.

anchor A bolt or rock used to fix a rope into a rock face

belay device A clip that attaches to a belayer's harness, through which a rope is fed

belayer The climber who guides the rope while belaying

bolt A metal bar that is screwed into the rock face to act as a permanent anchor

descender A braking device used to move down a rock face

fiberglass Material made from glass fibers

harness A belt with leg loops

grade A number that describes how difficult a rock face is to climb

Junior X Games An annual series of extreme sports competitions for kids aged 10-14

nut A metal wedge with a wire loop that is inserted in cracks on the rock face

rappel To descend by sliding down a rope

Roman numerals Any numbers formed with the characters I, V, X, L, C, D, and M

scrambling Moving up a steep hill while using the hands for balance

slings Looped nylon straps used to hook around rocky points and peaks

sponsorship An agreement in which a company pays athletes to promote its products

X Games An annual series of extreme sports competitions

INDEX

1 2 3 4 5 6 7 8 9 0   Printed in the U.S.A.   3 2 1 0 9 8 7 6 5 4